WHAT'S YOUR FAVORITE COLOR?

by Amber L. Lassiter

ISBN: 978-1-4834-9408-1 (sc)
ISBN: 978-1-4834-9409-8 (e)

Library of Congress Control Number: 2018913893

Lulu Publishing Services rev. date: 01/21/2019

DEDICATION

This book is dedicated to my parents the late William H. Lassiter, III and Michelle L. Copeland Lassiter. Both of you witnessed first hand the academic struggles I encountered. I remember how you both would stay up with me until 2:00 and 3:00 in the morning helping me to complete homework assignments. My parents never refrain from spending money on educational resources that would help me strengthen my academic skills. I have gleaned so much from your wisdom. I am proud that you both were my first teachers.

ACKNOWLEDGMENT

I want to thank my Aunt, Selma Copeland, brothers William H. Lassiter, IV and Michael Joseph Lassiter and sisters Aileen Lassiter, Sylvia Lassiter and Elizabeth Marnisha Lassiter for their support and encouragement throughout this entire process. Thank you for listening to me read my edits and revisions! Thank you for the suggestions and recommendations to improve the book. More importantly, thank you for always giving me words of encouragement. Your words of affirmation motivated me throughout this entire process. Thank you for helping me to transform a mere idea and dream into reality.

I want to thank Traci D. Anderson, who worked diligently as my editor. You strive to create a legacy of excellence in everything that you do. You carry out your legacy by positively impacting the lives of others, particularly through education. Your passion for instilling a love of life-long learning is helping to prepare children for a world we cannot even imagine. As a passionate educator, you have helped children develop self- confidence, learn from their own mistakes, grow spiritually as well as mentally. You have an intense dedication to culture and the recognition of what each of us has to contribute positively. Thank you for joining this journey with me.

Traci D. Anderson's mission has been to have a positive impact on the lives of others—particularly through education. She believes in setting strong foundations in today's children, as we prepare them for a world we cannot even imagine. To do so, she believes in instilling a love of life-long learning; belief in themselves and a willingness to learn from their own mistakes; a dedication to themselves—their spiritual as well as mental growth; ability to be critical thinkers and proactive problem solvers. Finally, she has a passionate commitment to culture and the recognition of what each of us has to contribute positively. Thank you for joining this journey with me.

I want to thank you Tangula Chambers for recommending Traci Anderson as an Editor. After I finished writing my manuscript, you helped me to find an editor. It has been a pleasure working with Traci, and I am thankful that you contacted Traci and my behalf and encouraged her to work with me.

Amal Bendriss, thank you for making graphic and typo revisions for me. Whenever I called you, you always availed yourself to help me in my time of need. Thank you for your willingness to help and your words of encouragement throughout this process.

I want to thank Mayor Andre Sayegh and First Lady Farhanna Balgahoom Sayegh for implementing a city-wide reading initiative for children. Thank you for being role models in our community and supporting the hard work and dedication of parents, mentors, and educators who are instilling a love for reading in children.

I want to thank my mentor Pastor Mitchell Green for helping me to understand the self-publishing process and encouraging me to publish my first book. Some of my other mentors from Paterson Public Schools and Seton Hall University are as follows: Mrs. Felisa Van Liew, Mr. Edward Cisneros, Ms. Richele Neal, Mr. Andre McCollum, Ms. Tyeisha Hilbert, Ms. Laurie Smith, Ms. Boblyn Dobbs, Ms. Grace Ayala, and Dr. Barbara Strobert. I am thankful because I have had the privilege of working with each of you in helping to strengthen our students' literacy skills. While working under your leadership, you allowed me to do what I love the most... that is to teach! None of you ever questioned my instructional practices or ideas. You never micromanaged me; you allowed me to make choices and decisions as I best sought fit to help our students excel. As a result, our students made significant academic gains.

I would like to thank one of my former teacher's, Ms. Julie Jackson. Ms. Jackson thank you for helping me to improve my writing skills in elementary school. You knew that I was a struggling writer, but you never dwelled on my weakness as a writer. You always highlighted my writing strengths. You worked tirelessly to help me strengthen my literacy skills. Now I am publishing my first book, so naturally, all your hard work has paid off. Thank you for being a passionate educator.

Amber was thrilled about going to school. Today students wore an article of clothing that represented their favorite color. Amber's teacher had told them that they were going to paint a picture using their favorite colors. When Amber entered her classroom, it didn't look or feel the way it usually did.

The windows were draped with long, sheer curtains in sunny yellow, cotton-candy pink, and ocean blue. They gently swayed back and forth from the cool breeze of the open windows. The glistening sun beamed through the curtains, reflecting the colors across the ceiling like a sparkling disco ball. The cheery colors made Amber feel warm, as if someone was giving her a bear hug.

Sounds of the wind whistled and echoed throughout the room. Amber closed her eyes. She puckered her lips together in an O shape and soft breaths exited her mouth mimicking the sounds of the wind.

When Amber opened her eyes, she noticed the banner on the wall: "Meet Our Picassos!" Under the banner were students' portraits, hanging horizontally inside of gold picture frames. Amber quickly glanced at a few of the portraits. Mrs. Lassiter had hung all twelve students' portraits in a specific order. First was Amber's! Beth's was second, and Crystal's was third. Liz's portrait hung before Michael's. William's portrait was after Michelle's, and Zion's portrait was the last picture on the wall.

Question: What can you tell about the order and pattern Mrs. Lassiter used to hang the students' portraits?

Hint: Write the order of students whose portraits were displayed to figure out the order and pattern Mrs. Lassiter used.

In the middle of the classroom, a white tarp covered the floor like sand on the beach. On top of the white tarp stood two rows of easels back to back. In front of each easel was a wooden stool, a smock, and a crocheted cotton beret. All students had an assigned workstation. The students ran to their easels and put on their smocks and crocheted cotton berets. Then, Amber and her classmates stood with stiff backs, like soldiers, while watching Mrs. Lassiter like hawks.

Mrs. Lassiter said, "Good morning, my little Picassos! Today is a special day. You all will paint a picture, and you must paint at least one item in your painting using your favorite color. I hope you all wore an article that matches your favorite color." Suddenly, Mrs. Lassiter raised her right hand in the air so it was parallel to her eye as she pointed her index finger toward the sky. "Everyone must keep their favorite color a secret until the masterpieces are revealed."

Amber was excited to begin painting. Unfortunately, she left her watercolors at home. Amber decided to go and borrow paint from the supply closet. She didn't want to use any of the paint colors that were in the closet, so she had no choice but to borrow paint from her classmates. She wanted to use some red paint but did not have any.

Question: In the sentence above it says, "Then Amber and her classmates stood with stiff backs, like soldiers, while watching Mrs. Lassiter like hawks. What does the author mean by "stood with stiff backs?"

Amber asked Michelle, "May I borrow some red paint?"

Michelle handed her the cherry-red can of paint, and then her eyes grew wide as if she had thought of a brilliant idea. "Aha! I bet red is your favorite color."

Amber's brows knitted in a frown. "I only asked for the red paint to finish my picture."

Michelle's face suddenly scrunched up as she folded her arms. "Red is your favorite color; that is why you wanted the red paint. I know you love red just like me!" Michelle snickered. "Don't worry; I won't tell anyone that red is your favorite color."

Amber decided to not a say another word to Michelle and went back to painting.

Questions: Why did Michelle think Amber's favorite color is red? Do you think Michelle believed Amber? How do you know? Why did Amber's brows knit into a frown?

After Amber added the red paint, she stood back and admired her work. "Hmmm, red looks beautiful, but I should add yellow. Yellow would liven up my picture. Ugh! I don't have any yellow paint."

Amber looked around the room and saw Michael with the banana-yellow paint can. "May I borrow some of your yellow paint, Michael?"

As Michael handed Amber the can, he started singing, "I know a secret; I know a secret!"

Amber loved secrets. She leaned toward Michael with her hand cupping her ear.

Question: Why did Amber lean toward Michael with her hand cupping her ear?

Michael twirled around Amber, singing louder. "I know a secret about Amber!"

Amber's head tilted to one, side and her mouth opened wide as she stared at Michael with wide eyes. She said curiously, "You know a secret about me?"

Questions: How did Amber feel when she found out Michael thinks he knows a secret about her? How do you know?

Michael's head bobbed. "Yup, sure do! Read my lips." Michael's lips moved in slow motion. "Your favorite color is *yellow*."

Amber's head moved slowly from side to side like a windshield wiper. "Michael, I just needed yellow to finish my painting."

"Uh-huh." Michael gave Amber a cocky wink. "Don't worry; I won't tell anyone our little secret."

Amber stared at Michael and then walked back to her workstation.

Questions: Why did Amber move her head slowly from side to side like a windshield wiper? Do you think Michael will keep the secret? How do you know?

Amber added the yellow paint to her painting; she stood back to admire her work. "Hmm, yellow looks beautiful, but I should add blue. Blue would liven up my painting. Oh, no! I can't believe that I do not have any blue paint." Amber noticed that Liz had some blue paint. "May I borrow some of your blue paint, Liz?"

Liz handed Amber the can of blue paint. "Oh, I betcha bl—"

Amber placed her index finger on Liz's lips. Then she sighed loudly as her eyes rolled up to the ceiling. Amber stomped her foot on the ground. "I needed some blue paint to finish painting my picture—that's all!" Amber took her index finger off of Liz's lips. Then she took a deep breath and slumped her shoulders.

Questions: What do you think Liz was going to say and why? How does Amber feel when she put her index finger on Liz's lips? How do you know? Why do you think Amber felt this way?

Liz put one hand on Amber's shoulder. "Geez! Take a deep breath. It's not my fault that I was smart enough to figure out blue was your favorite color. But your secret is safe with me." Liz squeezed her index finger and thumb together. Then she slid the fingers across her lips.

Amber decided to not say another word. She walked back to her easel with the blue paint. As Amber left, Liz slid her fingers back across her lips in the opposite direction.

Questions: What was Liz trying to do when she put one hand on Amber's shoulder? Why did Liz slide her fingers across her lips the first time? Do you think Liz can keep a secret? How do you know?

Amber added the blue paint and admired her work. She was quite pleased with her masterpiece. "Now, it's time to add my final touch. It's time to add my favorite color."

At that moment, Mrs. Lassiter announced, "All artists have ten minutes left to finish working. Then we will let our masterpieces dry. We will share them this afternoon."

Amber looked into her paint cans and realized that her favorite color paint was missing. "Oh no! What should I do now?" Amber's eyes scanned the room. She saw the other students placing their masterpieces near the windows to dry. Amber realized that everyone but her had finished painting.

Amber paced back and forth in front of her easel. "How can I show my work without my favorite color? Hmm, I could ask Selma to borrow paint." Amber looked slowly down toward the floor. "But if I ask Selma, then she will know my favorite color."

Amber went to the supply closet. "Maybe I can find my favorite color in the supply closet." But she couldn't find her favorite color paint in the supply closet. Amber walked back to her easel with her hands clasped behind her back. "What am I going to do?"

Mrs. Lassiter announced, "Five more minutes."

Amber sat on a stool with her face buried in her hands. "I guess I will have to show my masterpiece without my favorite color."

Question: Describe how Amber felt when she realized that she couldn't find her favorite color. What clues helped you to describe how Amber felt?

As Amber stood up to carry her portrait to dry by the window, she teetered and tottered like a baby learning how to walk. She knocked over the red and yellow paint cans on the edge of her easel. Amber bent down to clean the paint spill. As Amber wiped the red and yellow paints, they mixed together. A new color emerged! Amber snapped her fingers at her brilliant idea. "That's it!"

Amber dipped her paintbrush into the red and yellow paint cans. Then she dabbed her paintbrush onto the flower petals in her painting. She stood back to admire her work. The corners of her lips turned upward, and the front row of her teeth appeared. "Now, my beautiful masterpiece is completed."

"Amber, please put your masterpiece on the window sill to dry and line up for lunch," instructed Mrs. Lassiter.

Questions: How did Amber feel after she dabbed her paintbrush onto the flower petals? How do you know?

After lunch and recess, the paintings were all dry. Amber joined her classmates on the carpet. Michelle shared her painting first. Her portrait was all one color. The color she used rhymed with the word *bed*.

Next, Michael shared his painting. His favorite color rhymed with the word *bellow*.

Liz showed her painting. Her favorite color rhymed with the word *two*.

Then Amber shared her painting. "Ta-da! One of the flower petals is my favorite color."

Immediately, Michelle yelled, "Oh, her favorite color is red!"

"No, it's blue!" said Liz.

Michael swatted his hand like he was trying to hit a fly. "Her favorite color is yellow." Then Michael winked at Amber.

Questions: Why did Michael wink at Amber? How do you know?

"Oh, my goodness! Which is your favorite color—red, yellow, or blue?" asked Zion.

Amber shook her head. "None of these colors!"

Michelle, Michael, and Liz gasped.

"I wrote a riddle to help everyone figure out what my favorite color is." Amber read the riddle. "My favorite color is a color and the name of a piece of fruit."

Question: Based on Amber's riddle, what do you think is Amber's favorite color?

William shrugged. "You can't eat colors!"

Amber nodded at William. "You are right, William. *But*!" Amber paused and then clapped her hands together. The students' and Amber's eyes locked together. Amber's mouth widened, and the class leaned forward as they held their breath.

"You can eat an orange. Orange is my favorite color."

Liz's forehead crinkled. "Hey! What a minute! We all wore our favorite colors. You didn't!"

"Yes, Amber. That was a rule," said Mrs. Lassiter.

Amber smiled and shouted, "I did!" She lifted her pants legs. "I wore my favorite orange socks."

Question: What clues do the author and illustrator give to show Amber's favorite color?

AUTHOR BIOGRAPHY

Amber L. Lassiter lives in New Jersey. She has a Bachelor of Arts in Political Science, Master of Arts in Reading and a Master of Arts and Teaching in Elementary Education. Amber is currently pursuing an Educational Specialist degree (EdS) in Educational Policy, Management, and Leadership at Seton Hall University. She has worked as a classroom teacher, reading specialist, and literacy coach for fifteen years helping to transform reluctant readers into strategic confident readers. Amber enjoys bowling, singing karaoke music, listening to the saxophone and spending time with family and friends.

85309913R00020